Barnyard
Hullabaloo

You can read more stories about
the animals from Potter's Barn
by collecting the rest of the series.

For a complete list, look at
the back of the book.

Barnyard Hullabaloo

Francesca Simon

Illustrated by Emily Bolam

Orion
Children's Books

Barnyard Hullabaloo first appeared in *Moo Baa Baa Quack*,
first published in Great Britain in 1997
by Orion Children's Books
This edition first published in Great Britain in 2011
by Orion Children's Books
a division of the Orion Publishing Group Ltd
Orion House
5 Upper St Martin's Lane
London WC2H 9EA
An Hachette UK Company

3 5 7 9 10 8 6 4 2

A catalogue record for this book is available from the British Library.

ISBN 978 1 4440 0198 3

Printed in China

The Orion Publishing Group's policy is to use papers that are natural,
renewable and recyclable products made from wood grown in sustainable forests.
The logging and manufacturing processes are expected to conform
to the environmental regulations of the country of origin.

www.orionbooks.co.uk

For Nina Douglas

Hello from everyone

Moooo

Daffodil the cow

Rosie the calf

at Potter's Barn!

Father Goat

Bleat

Billy the Kid

Mother Sheep

Baaaaa

Tilly and Tam
the lambs

Mother Duck

Quack Quack

Five Ducklings

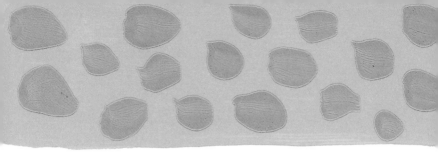

Neigh

Trot the horse

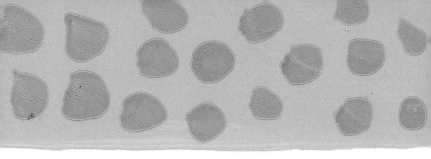

Honk
Honk

Gabby Goose

Woof

Buster the dog

Oink oink

Belle the pig

Cock-a-doodle-doo!

Red Roost

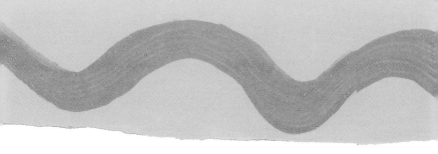

Squeaky the cat

Miaow

Henny-Penny

Cluck
Cluck

The chicks

Cheep
Cheep

Welcome to Potter's Barn!

The sun always shines and the fun
never stops at Potter's Barn Farm.
Join the animals on their adventures
as they sing, stomp, make cakes,
get lost, run off, and go wild.

"Cock a Doodle
Doo!"
"Cock a Doodle
Doo!"

It was morning at Potter's Barn.

The animals heard Red Rooster's
wake-up call, stretched their legs
and rose to start the day.

Someone hiding in Thistle Meadow
also heard Red Rooster crowing.

That someone was Fox.

"Hmmmmmmm,"
murmured Fox.
"Doesn't that Rooster
sound plump and juicy?"

He pricked up his ears
and listened again.

"Cock a Doodle Doo!"

"Cluck Cluck Cluck!"

"Cheep Cheep Cheep!"

"Ah yes," Fox added,
licking his sharp white teeth.

"Fine fat hens and chicks too.

I could fancy **a hen**…

…or **two**…

…or **three** for my dinner…

…with some tender little chicks
for dessert. Indeed I could."

Fox slunk through the long grass
of Thistle Meadow and peered
down at the farm.

"I think I'll pay Potter's Barn
a little visit tonight, heh heh heh."
And off he crept.

Buster was dashing round
Windy Haugh chasing squirrels
when suddenly he sniffed
a strange stinky whiff.

He raised his head and saw the
top of Fox's red tail bobbing in
and out of the grass.
Fox is back, thought Buster.
I'd better warn the others.

Meanwhile, the Potter's Barn
Band were rehearsing
a new song, "Barnyard Lullaby".
"Everyone ready?"
said Belle the pig.
"Let's take it from the top.
Ah-one, Ah-two…"

"Maaa Maaa"
"Baaaaa"
"Moooo Moooo!"
"Miaooooww!"
"Quack Quack!"
"Honk!"

bellowed
the animals.

"Stop! Stop!" shouted Belle.
"This is a lullaby.
Do you want to scare everyone?

Now let's try again,
softly this time.
Ah-one, Ah-two…"

"Watch out!"
barked Buster.

"Fox is about!"

Everyone was terrified.

"Ducklings! Stay close,"
quacked Mother Duck.

"What'll we do?
What'll we do?"
peeped the chicks, scurrying
under their mother's wings.

"I'll kick him," said Daffodil.

"I'll bite him," said Trot.

"I'll hide up the
oak tree and drop
down on him,"
said Squeaky.

"I'll butt him with my horns,"
said Billy the Kid.

Then Belle spoke.
"We want to frighten Fox
away for good," she said.
"And I've got an idea how."

The animals huddled together
and listened to Belle's plan.
"Agreed?" said Belle.
Everyone nodded.

Trot saw Fox first, sneaking
through the big woods.
He whinnied a warning.

"Neigh!"

Gabby saw Fox slither
into the orchard.
She shouted a warning.
"Honk! Honk!"

Buster saw Fox creep into the
farmyard, and head straight
for the hen house.
He barked a warning.
"Ruff! Ruff!
Ruff!"

Belle banged on a bucket.
"NOW!" she squealed.

"Barnyard
Hullabaloo!"

Maaaaaaaa

Mooooooooo

Ruff

Honk

Oink

Cluck Cluck
Cluck

Baaaa**aaaa**

Miaow

Quack
Quack

Neigh

roared the animals.

They screeched, they snarled, they yowled and they caterwauled.

They stomped their hooves
and clattered their heels,
shaking the ground.

Fox was so frightened that for a
moment he could not move.

Then he turned and ran,
yelping in terror.

"Help! Monsters! Help! Help!
Monsters at Potter's Barn!
Help! Save me!"

"Hurray!" cheered
the animals.

And from that day on,
Barnyard Hullabaloo has been
the Potter's Barn Band's favourite song.

As for Fox, he is still running.

Mmm
follow me

Did you enjoy the animals' Barnyard Hullabaloo? Can you remember the things that happened?

What does Red Rooster call to wake everyone up?

Who is hiding in Thistle Meadow?

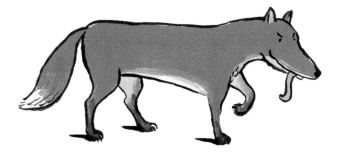

Why does Fox decide to pay
Potter's Barn a visit?

Who warns the other
animals about fox?

What does Daffodil the cow
say she'll do to Fox?

Who has an idea about how to
frighten Fox away for good?

Who spots Fox in the orchard?

What does Fox think is happening at Potter's Barn?

For more farmyard fun with the animals at Potter's Barn, look out for the other books in the series.

Where Are My Lambs?

Billy The Kid Goes Wild

Runaway
Duckling

Mish Mash
Hash

Chicks Just Want to Have Fun

Moo Baa Baa Quack